For Tara and Alexandra   KH
To Mary Craig with love   HC

VIKING
Published by Penguin Group
Penguin Young Readers Group, 345 Hudson Street, New York, New York 10014, U.S.A.
Penguin Group (Canada), 90 Eglinton Avenue East, Suite 700, Toronto, Ontario, Canada M4P 2Y3 (a division of Pearson Penguin Canada Inc.)
Penguin Books Ltd, 80 Strand, London WC2R 0RL, England
Penguin Ireland, 25 St Stephen's Green, Dublin 2, Ireland (a division of Penguin Books Ltd)
Penguin Group (Australia), 250 Camberwell Road, Camberwell, Victoria 3124, Australia (a division of Pearson Australia Group Pty Ltd)
Penguin Books India Pvt Ltd, 11 Community Centre, Panchsheel Park, New Delhi - 110 017, India
Penguin Group (NZ), Cnr Airborne and Rosedale Roads, Albany, Auckland 1310, New Zealand (a division of Pearson New Zealand Ltd)
Penguin Books (South Africa) (Pty) Ltd, 24 Sturdee Avenue, Rosebank, Johannesburg 2196, South Africa

Penguin Books Ltd, Registered Offices: 80 Strand, London WC2R 0RL, England

Angelina Ballerina © 1984 Helen Craig Ltd. and Katharine Holabird.
The Angelina Ballerina name and character and the dancing Angelina logo are trademarks
of HIT Entertainment Ltd., Katharine Holabird and Helen Craig. Reg. U.S. Pat. & Tm. Off.
First published in Great Britain by Aurum Press, 1984
First Published in the U.S. by Clarkson N. Potter, 1984
This edition published by Viking, a division of Penguin Young Readers Group, 2006
All rights reserved

1 3 5 7 9 10 8 6 4 2

Library of Congress Cataloging in Publication Data is available
ISBN: 0-670-06085-2

To find out more about Angelina, visit her Web site at www.angelinaballerina.com

Manufactured in China
Set in Bembo

Angelina
and the Princess

Story by **Katharine Holabird** Illustrations by **Helen Craig**

VIKING

Angelina was much too excited to sleep. The students at Miss Lilly's Ballet School had been asked to dance for Her Royal Highness, the Princess of Mouseland. Mr. Lightfoot, Director of the famous Royal Ballet Company, was coming tomorrow to help Miss Lilly choose the best ballerinas for the special performance. Angelina wanted a leading part so much that she worked on her pliés and pirouettes far into the night when she should have been sound asleep.

The next morning Angelina woke up feeling terrible. Her head ached and her ears buzzed. Angelina's mother took her temperature and shook her head sadly. "I'm afraid you'll have to stay in bed," she said. "You can't go to ballet school when you're not well."

But Angelina was determined to go. While her mother
was busy downstairs, Angelina packed her ballet bag...

...and tiptoed out of the house.

Angelina arrived at Miss Lilly's Ballet School just in time to join her friends Flora and Felicity and all the other ballerinas who were waiting to go onstage. Flora did a nimble leap and a delicate spin . . .

. . . and then it was Angelina's turn to dance. Her heart
started beating like a drum and she couldn't remember
what she was supposed to be doing.

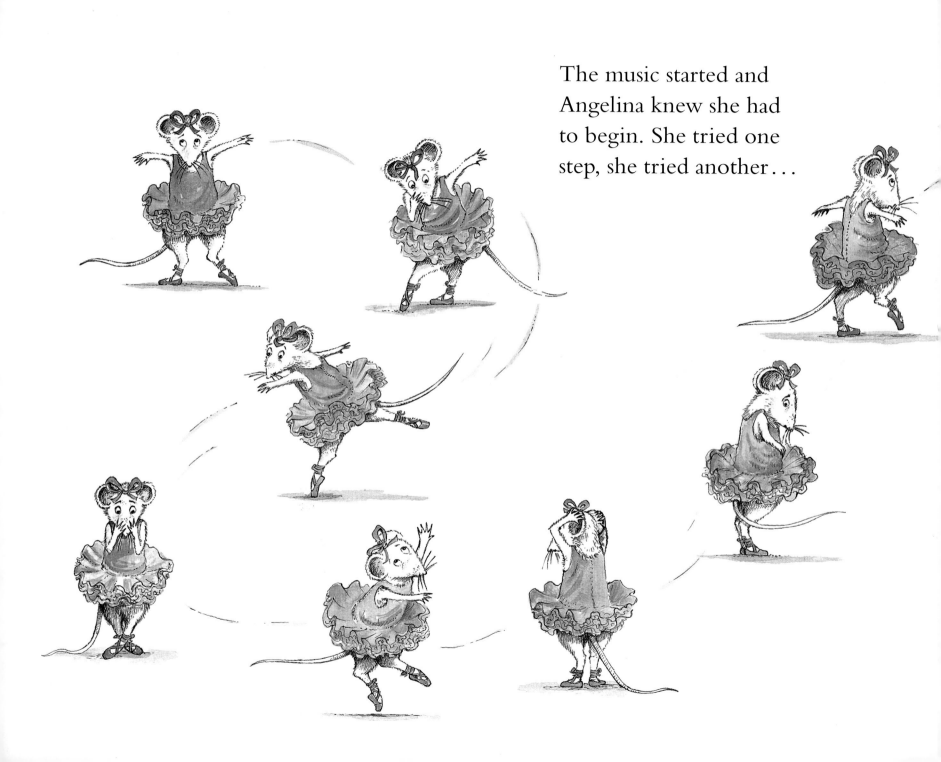

The music started and
Angelina knew she had
to begin. She tried one
step, she tried another...

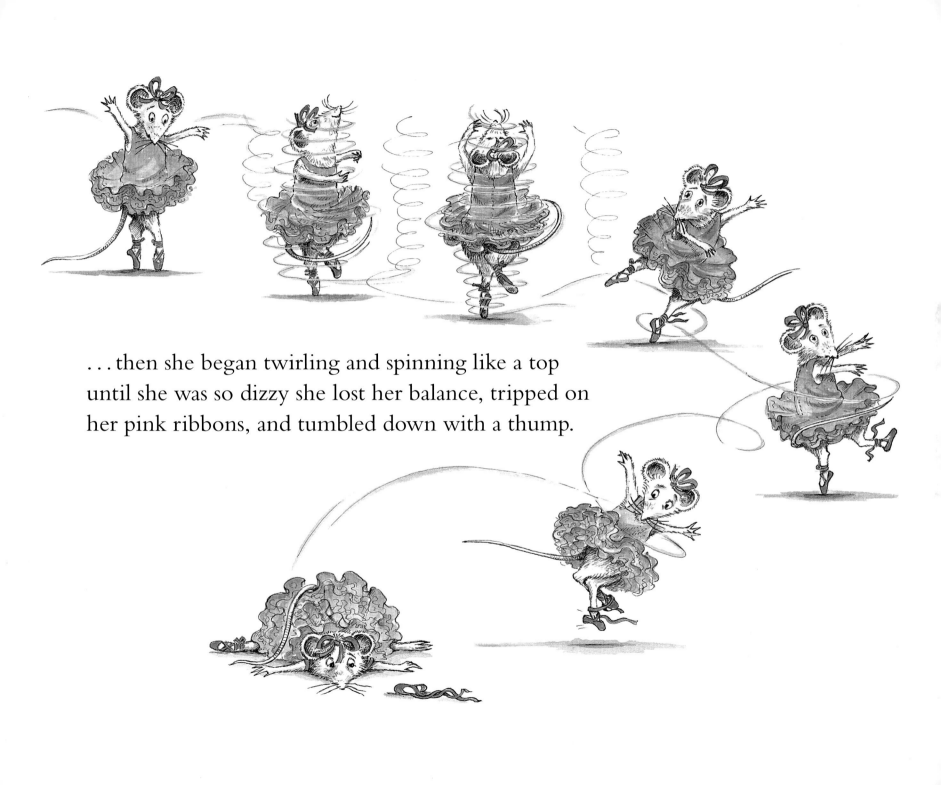

. . . then she began twirling and spinning like a top
until she was so dizzy she lost her balance, tripped on
her pink ribbons, and tumbled down with a thump.

Flora and Felicity were given the leading roles in the Dance of the Flower Fairies. Later, Miss Lilly called for Angelina. "I'm afraid you will have to take a smaller part this time," she said, trying to be kind.

When Angelina got home, her mother was very upset. "How could you run away like that when I told you to stay in bed?" she asked.

Angelina burst into tears. "I had to go to Miss Lilly's, but everything went wrong. I danced so badly for Mr. Lightfoot, I will never be a real ballerina. I am not going to ballet school any more."

Angelina's mother hugged her and kissed her and carried her upstairs, and in just a minute she was fast asleep in her own bed again.

The next day Angelina's headache was gone. She
felt better, but she was still very sad. "It's not fair!"
said Angelina.

"Maybe not," her mother said gently, "but things don't always go our way. You can still do your best with whatever part you are given, and that will help the whole performance."

Angelina thought about what her mother had said. Then she returned to Miss Lilly's after all, and rehearsed very hard with the other ballerinas for the Royal Performance.

After she had learned her own part, she memorized
the Dance of the Flower Fairies while watching
Flora and Felicity.

On the day of the Royal Performance, just as the show
was about to begin, Flora tripped and sprained her ankle.
Everyone was terribly upset.

Mr. Lightfoot and Miss Lilly turned to each other in horror. "Who can do the part?" they cried. Angelina was worried about Flora, but Susie stepped forward and said, "Angelina can!"

Angelina showed Miss Lilly that she had learned
the dance by heart. "But what about Flora?" she
asked. "Don't worry," said Miss Lilly, "we have a
treat for her...."

. . . So Flora was happy because she was invited to sit right next to the Princess of Mouseland. Mr. Lightfoot and Miss Lilly were happy because the performance could go on. Angelina was happy because she did the Dance of the Flower Fairies without forgetting a single step. The Princess of Mouseland was happy because she loved ballet.

When the performance was over she congratulated Angelina and thanked her warmly for saving the show.